Memphis and the Turtle

and the

Turtle

ANGELA GOFF

Archway Publishing books may be ordered through booksellers or by contacting:

Archway Publishing
1663 Liberty Drive
Bloomington, IN 47403
www.archwaypublishing.com
1 (888) 242-5904

Because of the dynamic nature of the Internet, any web addresses or links contained in this book may have changed since publication and may no longer be valid. The views expressed in this work are solely those of the author and do not necessarily reflect the views of the publisher, and the publisher hereby disclaims any responsibility for them.

Any people depicted in stock imagery provided by Thinkstock are models, and such images are being used for illustrative purposes only.
Certain stock imagery © Thinkstock.

ISBN: 978-1-4808-2328-0 (sc)
ISBN: 978-1-4808-2328-0 (hc)
ISBN: 978-1-4808-2330-3 (e)

Print information available on the last page.

Archway Publishing rev. date: 2/3/2016

I would like to dedicate this book to my grandson, Memphis. He gave me the inspiration to write this book and continues to be an inspiration in my life. He is a joy and a breath of fresh air in this world called life.

Love you,
Nana

I would also like to dedicate this book to my daughter, Katie. She inspires me to be a better mother and Nana.

Love you,
Mom

Once upon a time there was a little boy, named Memphis. Memphis and his mom and dad lived in a little town in Texas in a small housing edition at the edge of the woods. One day Memphis told his momma that he would like to go for a walk by the woods. She told him "do not go into the woods, Memphis". "I do not want you to get lost in the woods". Memphis said "ok, momma, I won't". He gave his momma a big hug and ran out the back door. He walked to the edge of the woods and started walking, looking at the ground and kicking rocks. After a while, he saw a turtle with his head poking out. He walked over to the turtle and all of a sudden the turtle snapped his head back into the shell. Memphis stood looking at the turtle for a long time, but the turtle would not poke his head back out. Memphis decided to continue on with his walk alongside of the woods. After Memphis walked for a while, he decided he had better return to his house before his mother started to worry about him.

Memphis came back upon the turtle, which had moved a little further along inside the woods. He was walking at a slow pace and did not see Memphis walk behind him. Memphis squatted down about a foot behind the turtle and asked him "Where are you going"? The turtle's head snapped back into his shell. Memphis said, "I won't hurt you". To Memphis' amazement, the turtle poked his head back out and looked at Memphis. The turtle said "I am going into the woods to find food". Memphis was so surprised the turtle spoke to him. He said, "I did not know turtles could talk". The turtle said, "We normally don't". "I am a special turtle". Memphis asked "What is your name?" and the turtle replied "my name is Ricket". Memphis said "Ricket"? I have never heard of anyone called Ricket before. Memphis said "my name is Memphis". The turtle said "I have never heard of anyone named Memphis". Memphis asked "Where is your momma" and Ricket replied "she left me one day about a year ago. She said I was old enough to be on my own". "She kissed me goodbye and then left". Memphis said "that is horrible!". "I would never want my momma to go away because I love her. Ricket said "in turtle life this is how it is done".

The turtle walked slowly along and Memphis followed him further into the woods. After a while, Memphis turned around and looked back. He could not see the edge of the woods. He remembered what his mother had told him about getting lost. Memphis just stood there looking around. He was not sure which direction to go to head back to his house. He asked Ricket "which way do I go to go back to the edge of the woods?" Ricket said "I don't know". Memphis began to get very upset and cry. Ricket said "what's wrong"? Memphis said "I don't remember how to get home". Ricket said "you can go with me and we can be friends". Memphis said, "But my momma will be mad at me if I don't go back". Ricket said, "Why would you want to go back and get into trouble?" Memphis thought about this for a while and decided to go with Ricket because he did not want to get into trouble or be alone.

They walked together for a long while and talked. It started to get dark in the woods and Memphis was beginning to get scared and began to cry. Ricket said "why are you crying?" Memphis said "I miss my momma and it is getting dark and I don't like the dark". Ricket said "when it gets dark I just hide in my shell". Memphis said "but if you hide in your shell, I will be alone". Ricket said "that is where I sleep". Memphis said "where am I going to sleep? I wanna go home" and he began to cry harder. Ricket tried to console Memphis but Memphis just sat down and cried harder. After a while, Memphis fell asleep and Ricket went into his shell.

When the light began to show at the top of the trees, Memphis woke up. He looked around confused. He did not know where he was. He looked around and saw the turtle eating leaves. Memphis said "I'm hungry" and Ricket said "do you want some of my leaves?" Memphis said, "I don't like leaves". Ricket said "I'm sorry". Memphis looked around and started to cry again. He said, "I want my momma". Ricket said, "I don't know where your momma is". Memphis cried harder. Ricket said, "Maybe you should walk back the way we came and go find your momma". Memphis said, "But I don't want to be alone; will you come with me"? Ricket said, "I need to go find water". Memphis said, "If you go with me and help me find my mother; we will give you all the water you need". Ricket thought about this for a while and then said, "Ok". Ricket did not want to lose his new friend, Memphis, so he decided to go back with him.

Memphis said, "Which way do we go?" Ricket said, "I don't' know". So Memphis decided to head out in the direction he thought they had come. They talked and talked about everything. Memphis liked his new found friend, Ricket. Ricket had never had a friend before and he really liked talking to Memphis. Their worlds were so different, but he enjoyed learning about Memphis' life. Memphis' mom sounded so wonderful. It would be nice to have a mother like his momma. Ricket was so excited to go to Memphis' house. He thought he would like it there very much and wanted a momma like Memphis had.

They walked and walked but they could not find the edge of the woods. Memphis was beginning to get worried that he would never find the edge of the woods. He did not remember walking this far into the woods. He knew his momma was going to be very angry at him for going into the woods, but he did not care, because he just wanted to see her so bad. He didn't care if she grounded him for a week; he just wanted to be home again. He didn't like it in the woods. It was scary. Thank goodness he had Ricket to talk to. He was so excited about his new friend. He couldn't wait to tell his momma about Ricket, if only he could get back home.

Memphis and Ricket walked and walked. What they did not know is that they were going further away from Memphis' house. Not further into the woods, but close to the edge of the woods. Memphis knew his momma would be worried when he did not return home. Maybe she would be so glad to see him that she would forget to punish him.

All of a sudden Memphis heard voices. He squatted down behind a log beside Ricket and whispered, "I hear people talking." "It doesn't sound like my mother". "Maybe we should hide until they go away". Ricket said, "Maybe it is people your momma knows, who are looking for you". Memphis said, "You think so?" Ricket said, "I don't know". "But you said she would be worried and maybe she is looking for you". Memphis decided to go toward the talking voices. If they looked bad, then maybe he could hide from them.

Memphis and Ricket walked closer and closer to the voices and when he got close enough to see one of the people; he noticed it was a man. He had some kind of uniform on. He didn't look scary and he was calling Memphis' name. Memphis came around a bush and said "My name is Memphis". The man walked over to Memphis and squatted down in front of him. He said, "Your momma is looking for you, son and is very worried about you". Memphis said, "You know my momma?" And the man said, "Yes, I do". "A bunch of people are looking for you". The man said, "My name is Butch". Memphis said, "Nice to meet you Butch". "Meet my friend, Ricket". "He walked with me so I wouldn't be lonely". I didn't tell Butch that Ricket talked to me; because I was afraid he would think I was crazy. Turtles are not supposed to talk, but my friend Ricket does.

Butch was a policeman and put Ricket and me in his car. It was exciting to ride in a police car. I think Ricket liked it too, but he would not talk to me, because he knew other people would not understand. Butch drove Ricket and me to my house. I was so excited to see my house and then my momma came running out of the house and opened the door and gave me a big hug. She was crying. I said, "why are you crying, momma?" She said, "I am so happy to see you Memphis. You had me scared to death". "I am so happy you are okay and home again". Memphis said, "I was so scared, momma". "I promise I will never go into the woods again".

I showed momma my new friend, Ricket. I asked her "Can Ricket come live with us?" She said "Sure he can." Ricket was happy too. He liked my momma instantly. He was so glad that she was not mad.

Memphis and Ricket lived very happily at his house. They played every day and never went into the woods again. Memphis and Ricket talked all the time, but Ricket never spoke in front of Memphis' parents. His talking was their secret.

New Books

Angela currently has other books to be published in the near future.

1. Memphis and the Hare – Be on the lookout for a continuation of Memphis' tale as he meets a Hare.
2. Ethan's Great Day – This book was inspired by Memphis' cousin, Ethan. This is another book to look for in the future.

Acknowledgements

I am deeply grateful to my daughter, Katie, for giving me feedback on the process of publishing this book. Her insight and ideas have helped me through the process.

A personal thank you to my husband, Bobby, for being patient with me on the long hours in front of the computer.

I am very thankful to Archway Publishing for making my dream a reality and making the process an easy one.

CPSIA information can be obtained at www.ICGtesting.com
Printed in the USA
BVOW10s0922250216

437869BV00023B/259/P

9 781480 823280

Memphis is a little boy who lives in little town in Texas. His house is near the woods, and he likes to go for walks. But his momma warns him not to go into the woods, or else he might get lost.

One day Memphis goes out for a walk and meets a turtle who is going into the woods. He is very surprised when he discovers that the turtle can talk! The turtle's name is Ricket, and he and Memphis become instant friends. Together they take a walk into the woods, where Ricket lives. But as it gets later and later, Memphis soon realizes that he is lost in the woods and doesn't know how to get home. Ricket doesn't know the way either. How will Memphis find his way home?

This children's story tells the tale of a little boy who meets a talking turtle and together they take an unexpected journey into the woods.

Angela Goff is a loving nana whose work is inspired by her two grandsons, Memphis and Ethan. Her writing career began with novels, but she soon realized her passion was in children's literature. She lives in Arlington, Texas, where she works as a writer and photographer.

U.S. $16.95

ISBN 978-1-4808-232

ARCHWAY
PUBLISHING

9 781480 823280

YOU ARE YOU AND YOU ARE GREAT

Melissa Marie